If Dogs Had Pockets

By Vic Parrish

Illustrated by Stephen Jackson

For more information contact:

Vic Parrish

Vic.parrish@yahoo.com

ISBN-13: 987-1484124321

ISBN-10: 1484124324

For additional copies please contact the author as above.

ACKNOWLEDGEMENTS

To Lori, Frona and River, who daily fill my pockets with love VP

I dedicate the drawings to all caring people who have rescued or will rescue dogs (or any other animals for that matter) SJ

HAVE YOU

EVER

WONDERED...?

If dogs had pockets, then what would they keep?

Once this thought struck me when I was asleep.

If dogs had pockets, then what would they keep?

Perhaps some mementos from lives that are deep.

If dogs had pockets, then what would be there?

I bet mine would keep just a bit of cat hair

From the neighborhood tabby that sleeps on the stair –

Or maybe a bit of a chocolate éclair.

If dogs had pockets, then what would they stash?

I wonder if puppies would have need for cash?

To buy a blue ribbon, or maybe a sash?

I bet a dog's spending would be rather rash.

If dogs had pockets, then what would they own?

I think you'll agree they would all keep a bone

Or maybe a chew toy for when they're alone.

Or this would be funny – a dog with a phone!

With phone in its pocket a dog could call friends

To ask for the payback of money it lends

Or maybe to warn of some frightening winds

Or keep up to date with the latest dog trends.

Many dogs like to stay out late at night –

A pocket is perfect to keep a flashlight.

Dogs in the day get their light from the sun;

Their pockets would have room for things that are fun.

Perhaps a dog might keep some kibble it saved

Or pads for its feet for the road that is paved.

A old piece of cloth as a flag could be waved

To ensure that a dog who was lost could be saved!

A dog might keep something to help when it ate

Like maybe some sodium bicarbonate.

A smart pooch might find an old key to a gate

To gobble the neighbor cat's food when it's late.

With pocketed mask 'twould be easy to fool

The teachers, so it could sneak into the school

To be with its master – now that would be cool!

To keep a dog waiting all day can be cruel.

What if a dog had a map to a lake

So when it got hot a nice swim it could take?

While splashing around oh what noise it would make!

As the rest of us worked – wouldn't that take the cake?

If dogs had pockets you know they'd get lint.

Would they keep crystals in light that would glint?

What about fire – could they start one with flint?

Not that they'd burn things. That's not what I meant.

A dog might keep scissors so it could cut stuff

Like cat hair and leashes and furniture fluff.

But if it kept cutting then things could get rough!

A dog has to know when enough is enough.

The sneakiest doggies would have tennis shoes

To stay oh so quiet when they creep up on you.

The noisiest doggies who holler and yell

Would want to keep room for a whistle and bell.

I've seen a dog chasing a car down a road -

Could a dog's pocket contain such a load?

What is the reason they'd run such a race?

To keep any of it they'd need a suitcase.

If dogs had pockets they'd keep many things

Like dirtballs and branches and shiny gold rings.

They might keep some medicine 'cause they get stings.

I think then that dogs would be richer than kings!

A dog might keep something to help it run faster –

The list of the things that they'd keep is much vaster,

Including the love that they have for their master.

If dogs had pockets, they'd keep what they haster!

Made in the USA
Charleston, SC
22 April 2013